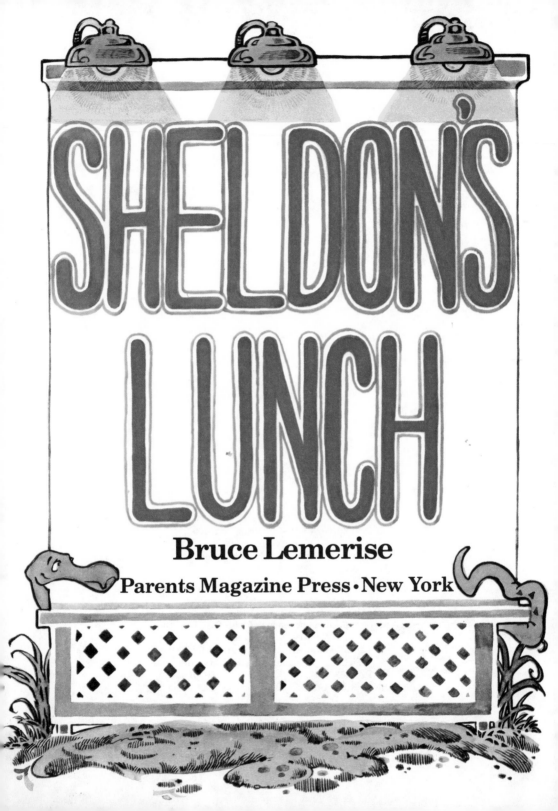

SHELDON'S LUNCH

Bruce Lemerise

Parents Magazine Press • New York

Copyright © 1980 by Bruce Lemerise.
All rights reserved.
Printed in the United States of America.
10   9   8   7   6   5   4   3

Library of Congress Cataloging in Publication Data
Lemerise, Bruce. Sheldon's lunch.
SUMMARY: Sheldon has more than enough pancakes for
his own lunch but not enough for his friends, so they
proceed to make more.
[1. Pancakes, waffles, etc.—Fiction. 2. Cookery—
Fiction. 3. Animals—Fiction] I. Title.
PZ7.L53737Sh   [E]   80–10449
ISBN 0–8193–1025–5 ISBN 0–8193–1026–3 lib. bdg.

This book is dedicated to
my mother, MARIE LEMERISE,
who was always there
to fix my lunch.

Sheldon's mother was busy
making blueberry pancakes.
They were Sheldon's favorite.

"I have to go shopping," she said.
"Be good and clean up after
you're finished. Enjoy your lunch."

Sheldon sat down at the table.
He flipped pancakes one by one
in the air, catching them
in his mouth.

Suddenly, Sheldon heard a noise
behind him. He turned around
and saw his friends at the window.
"Mmm. Those pancakes look good,"
they said. "They probably
taste good, too."
There were more pancakes than
Sheldon could eat by himself,
so he invited his friends in.

They all began to eat.
"Blueberry pancakes are my favorite,"
said Oscar Raccoon.
"Mine, too," said Sheldon.

"I'm all finished, but I'm
still hungry," said Oscar.
"Me, too," said Randy Owl.
"More, please!" cried
Billy Frog and Chuck Bear.

"I've cooked many things,
but never pancakes," said Sheldon.
"They look easy enough, though."

Sheldon read from the cookbook.

Makes about twenty 2½-inch pancakes

2 cups all-purpose flour
1 teaspoon salt
1 teaspoon baking soda
2 eggs, slightly beaten
2 cups buttermilk
2 tablespoons melted butter or
    margarine
1 pint blueberries

Then he got to work.

Stir together the flour,
salt, and soda.
Add the eggs, milk, and butter.
Stir till just moist.
Mix in blueberries.

"Wait a minute," said Chuck.
"If blueberries are good
in pancakes, then how about
cinnamon, ginger, and honey?
I'm going to add some of each."

"This doesn't look like enough
batter," said Randy. "I think
it needs more flour and milk.
And I'll add some yeast, too.
That will make it grow!"

And then Oscar said,
"Don't forget marshmallows,
fudge, and cream!"

Billy looked on all the kitchen shelves
and came back with his arms full.
"I like a little bit of everything,"
he said.

The mixture began to grow

and grow.

The batter began to shake.

Then suddenly it spilled over
the edge of the bowl ...
all around the kitchen.
"Oh, no!" cried Randy.
"Look out!" yelled Sheldon.
"We're doomed!" screamed Oscar.

Everyone was covered from head to foot in thick, gooey batter!

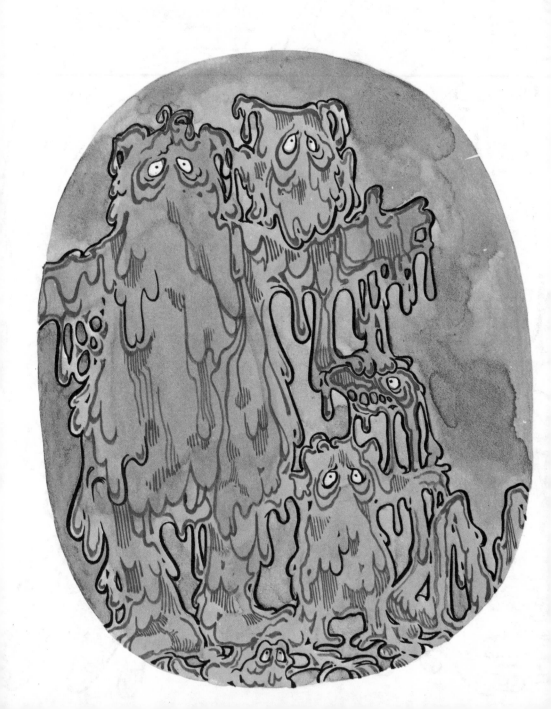

"Now we'll make pancakes
the right way," said Sheldon.
"First we'll clean ourselves up."
Sheldon was covered so thickly
that Oscar had to scrape
the batter off him.

"Now we'll clean up the mess!"
Sheldon continued.

Randy flapped about,
directing the clean-up.

Chuck scraped off batter
from all the high places.

Oscar scooped up batter
from all the low places.

Billy hopped around,
throwing away the garbage.

And Sheldon
swept,

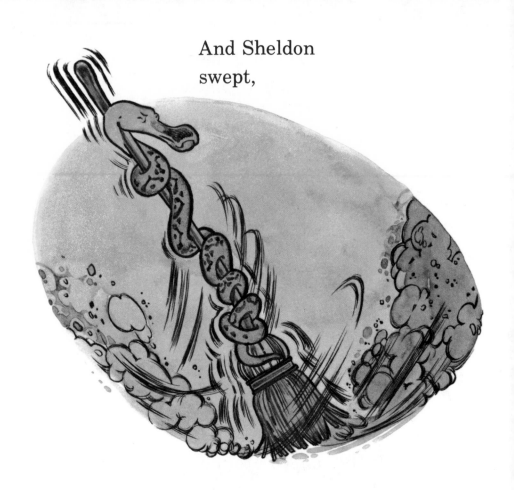

scrubbed,

and cleaned

until everything was spotless.

Sheldon and his friends had
all they wanted to eat.

And they all helped wash up.

Just as they finished,
Sheldon's mother
returned from shopping.

She put away her packages
and called to Sheldon
in the kitchen.
"Sheldon, did you have
a nice lunch?"

And Sheldon and his friends
called back ...

WE ALL HAD A
GREAT LUNCH!

PLEASE
TURN THE PAGE
FOR THE COMPLETE
RECIPE.

Makes about twenty 2½-inch pancakes

2 cups all-purpose flour
1 teaspoon salt
1 teaspoon baking soda
2 eggs, slightly beaten
2 cups buttermilk
2 tablespoons melted butter or
    margarine
1 pint blueberries

Stir together the flour,
salt, and soda.
Add the eggs, milk, and butter.

Stir till just moist.
Mix in blueberries.

Drop batter by scant 1/4 cupfuls
onto hot, lightly greased griddle.
(Don't crowd pancakes.)

Cook over medium heat
until top of pancake is bubbly
and bottom is golden brown.

Turn pancakes and brown other side.
(To flip pancakes, give turner
a sudden lift and tilt—
up and over!)

When pancakes are cooked,
keep them ready to eat by
placing them in shallow pan
in warm oven.

Make more pancakes using
rest of batter.

ABOUT THE AUTHOR/ARTIST

Bruce Lemerise says, "As long as I remember, I was interested in two things: drawing and snakes. As a boy, I went on snake hunts to find as many snakes as I could for my collection. At one time I had ten garter snakes, a corn snake, a water snake, and a baby decay snake. I could never understand why people were afraid of them. Finally owning a six-foot boa constrictor was a dream come true!"

Mr. Lemerise credits both his parents for getting him started in his career. Since art school, his work has included Broadway posters and greeting cards. This is his first children's book.